Greystone Kids / Greystone Books Ltd.
greystonebooks.com

Cataloging data available from Library and Archives Canada
ISBN 978-1-77164-713-7 (cloth)
ISBN 978-1-77164-714-4 (epub)

Editing by Chelene Knight, President of Breathing Space Creative Literary Studio
Art and text consultation by Aisha Kiani, founder of I Dream Library
Copy editing by Alicia Chantal
Proofreading by Doretta Lau
Jacket and interior design by Sara Gillingham Studio
Printed and bound in China on FSC®-certified paper at Shenzhen Reliance Printing.
The FSC® label means that materials used for the product have been responsibly sourced.
The illustrations in this book were rendered in paper collage.

Greystone Books thanks the Canada Council for the Arts, the British Columbia Arts
Council, the Province of British Columbia through the Book Publishing Tax Credit,
and the Government of Canada for supporting our publishing activities.

Greystone Books gratefully acknowledges the xʷməθkʷəy̓əm (Musqueam),
Sḵwx̱wú7mesh (Squamish), and səlilwətaɬ (Tsleil-Waututh) peoples on
whose land our Vancouver head office is located.

IMAGINE A GARDEN

STORIES OF COURAGE
CHANGING THE WORLD

BY **RINA SINGH**

ART BY
HODA HADADI

GREYSTONE KIDS

GREYSTONE BOOKS • VANCOUVER / BERKELEY / LONDON

FOR ANGAD AND LAINY,
WITH LOVE —R.S.

A GARDEN OF GRENADES

Along the Mediterranean Sea,

where the sun shines boldly

on a piece of divided land,

rockets and grenades

keep war alive on both sides.

Close to the fence,

in the village of Bil'in,

tear gas grenades fall

like a meteor shower.

Trailing white fumes seize

lungs,

sting eyes.

When the clouds of smoke evaporate

and coughs and cries subside,

a mother picks up the canisters of spent grenades

and fills them with earth.

She plants flowers in them—red, white, pink.

Unlike tears,

water does not flow freely here.

So, she measures the water carefully and gives the flowers

just enough to survive.

Children walk by her garden and wonder

if this is what peace looks like.

THE BALLET TEACHER

Perched on Rio's rolling hills,

with a view of mountains

and the ocean,

is the sprawling neighborhood of Alemão.

Bullies patrol with rifles

spreading danger

in the maze of its sloped streets.

In an abandoned basketball court

on top of a hill,

a young woman stretches.

Forty-nine little girls stretch with her.

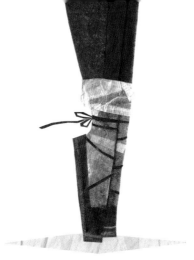

She pauses the music to straighten their arms.

She teaches

them to stand perfectly on their toes.

She tells them about the world.

She offers them

a hope, a dream, a better chance

to be whoever they want to be.

When there is shooting nearby, she stops the music.

She tells them to lie low and be quiet.

When it's over, she tells them to get back on their toes.

And they do. They dance,

trampling the sounds of fear

beneath their feet.

THE LESSON

Every eight minutes,
a train roars over a bridge in Delhi.
Under the bridge, the ground rumbles.
The children don't mind the noise.
They come in shifts—
sons and daughters
of migrant workers,
rickshaw pullers,
daily wage laborers—
and sit cross-legged on the dirt floor
to practice words from the chalkboard
painted on the wall.

They solve sums.

They draw pictures.

They ask questions.

Their school has no chairs, no desks, no other walls.

The pillars mark its boundary.

The bridge protects them from sun and rain.

They sit wide-eyed and listen to their teacher.

He has already taught them

they belong in school—

the only lesson they need to learn

for now.

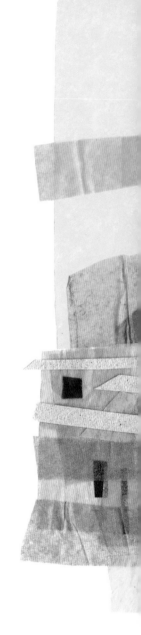

THE COACH

Against the backdrop of a mountain,
its straight edge softened by the African sun,
lies Khayelitsha—a township
on the outskirts of Cape Town.
A football lover arrives from afar
looking for a future.
Jobless and disheartened,
he rolls up an old jersey and some plastic bags
and ties the rag ball with a string.
He dribbles it in a sandy field
packed between streets and settlements.

Before he knows it, boys show up

calling him: Coach.

They clap. They sing.

They stamp their feet in dance.

They learn to kick the lopsided ball

into makeshift goalposts made of tree branches.

He offers no dreams

of rags-to-riches fame—

only a ball and a pitch.

One becomes faith, the other a classroom.

This is how he leads them

beyond the game.

THE WATER PROTECTOR

In the world's largest freshwater lake

lies Manitoulin Island

where life and legend,

time and water flow together.

An eight-year-old girl

attends a water ceremony in a community

that has murky water.

She is shocked to learn from her mother

that the children

from hundreds of communities

don't know what a drinking tap is.

They see water

trucked to their homes

and boiled in large pots

while companies pump water from their land

and bottle it for profit.

She learns

of the betrayal of leaders

and grows up carrying

the burden of thirst

of her people.

She begins to speak at world events

and her voice roars across nations.

She tells the adults who run this world:

We can't eat money or drink oil—

Water is sacred; water is life

It's time to warrior up and save what we have.

As if they should need

reminders.

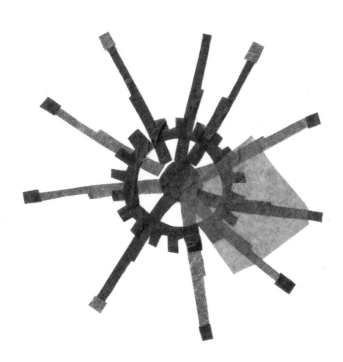

IMAGINE

In Mexico City,

where the bustling streets rest

on the grid of Aztec ruins,

it is here, an artist waits,

as the city dismantles

6,700 illegal weapons

and gives him the metal remnants.

He brings them to his studio,

lays them out,

moves parts around,

and rearranges them.

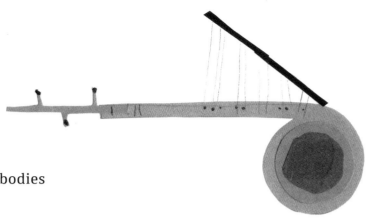

He imagines shapes that can be bodies
to musical instruments.
He looks at guns, pistols, rifles.
He sees flutes, guitars, saxophones.
He invites technicians
to hammer, fuse, solder, and string.
He makes a marimba, a flute, and a xylophone from the barrels
and a guitar from the handguns.

He asks musicians to extract sounds
from the instruments,
play the notes,
and form an orchestra.
In galleries and museums,
around the world,
he shows that even the instruments of death
can be healed by art.

MAMA MARIA

The island of Samos
with forested mountains
and pebbled beaches
lies in the turquoise waters
of the Aegean Sea.
A woman watches from her seaside restaurant
as strangers disembark from rafts, boats.

Men. Women. Babies.

Wet. Hungry.

She thinks of her own refugee mother
eating bread, dipped in water,
sprinkled with sugar.

She invites them in,
offers them vegetables, rice,
soup, bread.

The tourists stay away.

Her local customers stop coming.

They fear strangers—their scarves, their prayers.

She gets anonymous calls:

Stop helping them or we'll hurt you.

She closes the restaurant and cooks from her kitchen at home—

thousands of meals over months.

Men hug her and call her mama.

Women sing songs for her.

Children pay her with drawings

of boats, birds, and hearts.

If she ever runs out of food,

she promises,

she will still give them love.

ABOUT THE STORIES

A GARDEN OF GRENADES

In the village of Bil'in, near the West Bank city of Ramallah, Sabiha Abu Rahmah, a Palestinian mother, collected canisters of used tear gas grenades and turned them into flowerpots. In 2009, she lost her son in the ongoing Israeli-Palestinian conflict. With no shortage of materials, she has placed the grenades in rows to create a garden in memory of her son.

THE BALLET TEACHER

Tuany Nascimento, a young gymnast and a dancer in Rio de Janeiro, Brazil, gave up her own dream of becoming a professional ballerina because her family needed her to provide for them. She took an office job and rehearsed ballet in her spare time. In her favela, a low-income neighborhood where poverty has driven some to crime, little girls watched with great interest. In 2012, she started *Na Ponta dos Pes – On Tiptoes*, free ballet classes for girls ages 4–14. Dancing in ballet costumes, these girls must be enrolled in a school with passing grades in order to learn to dance. She teaches them to dream of a life beyond their dangerous streets.

THE LESSON

Rajesh Sharma, a grocery store owner in Delhi, India, wanted to become an engineer but his family could not afford to send him to college. In 2006, standing by a bridge, he noticed children playing in a construction zone during school hours. When he asked the migrant workers why their children were not in school, they said the school was too far. He decided to teach a few kids for two hours a day for free. His school survives on donations of notebooks, mats, and snacks from private citizens. More than a decade later, there are more than two hundred children who come to what is called "Free School Under the Bridge" which is literally under a subway bridge.

THE COACH

Dumisani Madondile, a football enthusiast, arrived in Khayelitsha, South Africa, in 1996, looking for a better life. After struggling for years, one day he made a rag ball and started kicking it around in a field. Boys came to play the game—also known as soccer—and stayed to become responsible citizens and leaders of their community. For years, Coach Dumi, as he is affectionately called, has been working hard to keep the boys in school. The rag balls have been replaced with limited numbers of real footballs. But what has not changed is that the boys of the township still love, live, and breathe football.

THE WATER PROTECTOR

Autumn Peltier is an Anishinaabe water activist from the Wiikwemkoong First Nation on Manitoulin Island in Northern Ontario, Canada. She was eight years old when she attended a water ceremony in the Serpent River First Nation community and learned they and hundreds of other communities had no access to safe water. That day she decided to become an advocate for clean drinking water for Indigenous communities across Canada. Canada is the most water-rich country in the world and yet, even there, people's access to water is still at risk. Inspired by her mother and her aunt, Josephine Mandamin, who was known as Grandmother Water Walker, Autumn has fought for water rights and traveled all over the world to educate people about the sacredness and the importance of clean water. At the age of fourteen, she became the Chief Water Commissioner for the Anishinaabek Nation.

IMAGINE

Pedro Reyes is an award-winning experimental artist from Mexico, who is on a mission to end gun violence through creativity. In one of his earlier projects, *Palas por Pistolas* (Shovels for Guns), he melted guns to make shovels. He then distributed them to public schools and art institutions for community members to use them for planting trees. He sees his studio as a laboratory because he experiments with ideas to change the world. Art and action go hand in hand for him. In 2012, he held an exhibition of fifty playable musical instruments, which he made out of 6,700 donated revolvers, shot guns, and machine guns. His project was called *Imagine*.

MAMA MARIA

In 2015, on the Greek island of Samos, Maria Makrogianni welcomed refugees
to her restaurant. People fleeing the civil war in Syria came via Turkey by the
thousands seeking shelter in Greece. They planned to stay a short while on the
island before getting approval to move to the mainland and then on to other
European countries to start new lives. But, that didn't happen as many countries
closed their borders. Some local people were afraid their way of life would
be changed by the presence of refugees. When Maria got threatening phone
calls, she closed her restaurant and cooked from home. After hearing her story,
people from around the world donated money to keep her pantry full. The
refugees affectionately call her Mama Maria.

AUTHOR'S NOTE

Our world is not always an easy place to live in. There is war, poverty, and violence in many parts of our planet. The news mostly puts a spotlight on what is wrong with our world. But there is a lot that is right too. There are people who get out of bed every morning and spend their days thinking of others and making things better for their communities.

This book is a tribute to some of those everyday heroes—a mother, a dancer, a teacher, a coach, a teenager, an artist, and a restaurant owner who show tremendous courage and creativity to calm fears and foster hopes, making their world a little safer, a little better, and a lot happier.

These stories happening around the globe showed me that changing the world does not require daring acts of bravery. We don't have to end wars or find cures to terrible diseases, but we do have to put other people first. Even our smallest actions can be world changing. I hope you are inspired to reimagine your world through the lens of love and kindness as well.

—*Rina Singh*

LET IT GROW

by Mary Ann Fraser   illustrated by Riley Samels

CAPSTONE EDITIONS
a capstone imprint

Published by Capstone Editions, an imprint of Capstone
1710 Roe Crest Drive
North Mankato, Minnesota 56003
capstonepub.com

Library of Congress Cataloging-in-Publication Data
Names: Fraser, Mary Ann, author. | Samuels, Riley, illustrator.
Title: Let it grow / by Mary Ann Fraser ; illustrated by Riley Samuels.
Description: North Mankato, Minnesota : Capstone Editions, an imprint of Capstone, [2021]
Audience: Ages 5–7. | Audience: Grades K–1.
Summary: A child learns about the life cycle of a giant pumpkin and the rewards of letting it grow.
Includes "Pumpkin Fun Facts" and information on growing and racing giant pumpkins.
Identifiers: LCCN 2021002347 (print) | LCCN 2021002348 (ebook) | ISBN 9781684463800 (hardcover)
ISBN 9781684463770 (ebook pdf) Subjects: CYAC: Pumpkin—Fiction.
Life cycles (Biology)—Fiction. | Patience—FIction. Classification: LCC PZ7.F86455 Le 2021 (print)
LCC PZ7.F86455 (ebook) | DDC [E]—dc23
LC record available at https://lccn.loc.gov/2021002347
LC ebook record available at https://lccn.loc.gov/2021002348

Image Credits: Shutterstock: Cindy Bird, (pumpkins), Italarico (pumpkin race)

Designed by Nathan Gassman

Printed and bound in China. 004205

WHAT DO YOU HAVE IN YOUR HAND?

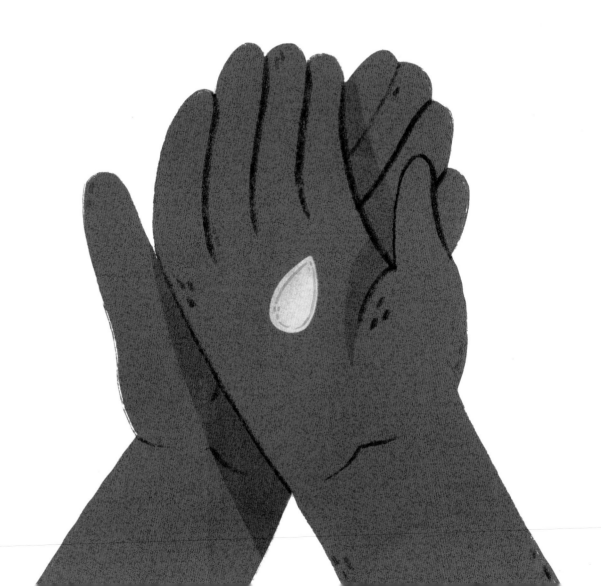

A seed.
A very special seed.

ARE YOU GOING TO EAT IT?

Oh no!
I'll let it grow.

I'll push the seed into the dirt, water it, and yank any weeds until a sprout pokes its head up.

AND THEN YOU'LL PLUCK THE LEAFY
SPROUT AND ADD IT TO A SALAD?

Oh no!
I'll let it grow.

The sprout will creep and twine this way and that
until a blossom the color of marmalade appears.

AND THEN YOU'LL PICK THE FLOWER
FOR A BOUQUET?

Oh no!
I'll let it grow.

The flower will yawn open until a bumbling bee dusted in pollen
drinks from the flower and makes it fruit.

AND THEN YOU'LL MUNCH
THAT FRUIT FOR A SNACK?

Oh no!
I'll let it grow.

The fruit will turn from green to gold
and swell until it is a sweet, baby pumpkin.

AND THEN YOU'LL PICK THE SWEET,
BABY PUMPKIN TO MAKE A PIE?

Oh no!
I'll let it grow.

The baby pumpkin will drink up buckets of water
and soak up the sun's rays until it is as
plump and orange as a basketball.

AND THEN YOU WILL CARVE THAT
PLUMP PUMPKIN INTO A JACK-O'-LANTERN?

AND THEN—LET ME GUESS—
YOU'LL LET IT GROW SOME MORE?

Oh no!

I'll saw that giant pumpkin right off the vine.
With lots of help, I will roll it up a plank and onto a truck.

TO HAUL IT TO MARKET?

Oh no!
I'll take it to the fair!

The judges will weigh the giant pumpkin, and maybe it will win a prize.

Oh no!

I'll cut a giant hole in my giant pumpkin and scoop out all the seeds.

WILL YOU THROW THE REST AWAY?

Oh no!

With brushes and lots of paint
we'll fancy up the hollow pumpkin.

Then we'll launch it into the lake.

WON'T THE PUMPKIN SINK?

Oh no!
It will float like a boat!

We'll grab some paddles, hop on in,
and sail it in the Great Pumpkin Regatta.

AND THEN TO CELEBRATE YOU'LL ROAST
AND EAT THAT PLENTIFUL PILE OF SEEDS?

Oh no!
Next year we'll let them ALL grow.

Growing and Racing Giant Pumpkins

Growing giant pumpkins for competition began with William Warnock of Ontario, Canada, in the early 1900s. For 76 years, he held the world record for the largest pumpkin. Then along came Howard Dill.

Dill was a farmer from Nova Scotia, Canada. He created the Atlantic Giant pumpkin, which broke Warnock's record in 1979. Dill's giant pumpkins began winning competitions all around the world. People wanted to buy Atlantic Giant seeds to grow and develop their own giant pumpkins.

When Howard died, his son, Danny Dill, took over the farm. One day a woman asked what else they could do with the giant pumpkins. Danny decided they could race them!

That was the beginning of the Windsor Pumpkin Regatta, which takes place each year on Lake Pesaquid in Windsor, Nova Scotia. Thousands of people flock to Windsor every October to watch the half-mile race. This race has inspired other pumpkin regattas around the world.

West Coast Giant Pumpkin Regatta in Tualatin, Oregon

Plentiful Pumpkin Facts

- The first pumpkins grew wild and were only the size of a baseball.

- Pumpkins have been growing in North and Central America for thousands of years, with the oldest seeds found in Mexico.

- Pumpkins are a fruit and belong to the same food family as squash, cucumbers, watermelons, and melons.

- You can eat every part of a pumpkin, including the skin, leaves, flowers, pulp, seeds, and stem!

- The word *pumpkin* comes from the Greek word *pepon*, which means "large melon."

- There are more than 45 different kinds of pumpkins.

- Pumpkins are grown on every continent except Antarctica.

- Giant pumpkins are the heaviest fruits in the world. As they grow, they can gain 20 to 40 pounds (9 to 18 kilograms) a day!

- In 2016, Mathias Willemijns from Belgium grew a pumpkin that weighed 2,624.6 pounds (1,190.5 kg), which is more than some cars weigh!

- Atlantic Giant pumpkins are the most common type of pumpkins grown for world-record competitions.